"The Water Cycle's tiniest worker... ...with the biggest fears!"

Larry
Breaks The Cycle

Written/illustrated by:
Eevee Gracie Maribelle

"Larry Breaks The Cycle"
all rights reserved
Copyright © Ashley
Mills/ DBA Eevee Gracie
Maribelle 2024

WATER, WATER...

drip

                spill

                              splashin'

LETS LOOK REAL CLOSE..

                              SEE THEM IN ACTION

Look at how hard they're working!
They're as busy as can be!

The Water Cycle is a special job!
...ALWAYS RECYCLING.

Let's see if we can find them!
Our friends-Claude, the Sun, and Mary!

And of COURSE we cannot forget
Our **new** friend, little Larry!

The SUN has a BIG BIG role!
with a smile so warm and bright.

There, I see Mary, getting ready for her flight.

Phase 1, Evaporation.
when the sun warms up the ground.

The liquid is changed to vapor...

flying up high

Mary says, " just DON'T LOOK DOWN!"

She sure moved fast.

She's up there with Claude for the next phase, they wait.

As others arrive, she says to Claude...

"WHERE'S LARRY? HE'S RUNNING Late!"

"I know he sometimes hides."
Said Claude.
He has some real bad fears...poor Larry!"
"But we need to tell him it's OK!
And all the things
That WE find scary!

"I get SO NERVOUS!
"Learning to ride my bike." .
Said Mary!

"That's why
PRECIPITATION'S hard too!
It's the FALLING I find scary"

Claude said, "For me, I'm scared of storms.
They're way too bright and loud!"

"..I know that seems kinda silly
well, you know, since I'm a cloud."

"I'm afraid of the dark."
Sun said.
"...a room or a BIG DARK PLACE!"

"But do y'all know where I live?!
Up there in **OUTER SPACE!**"

"Hey, look! Here comes Larry!"
He sure looks worried..."

"I am! I FEEL SICK 'CAUSE IT'S ALL SO SCARY!"

Claude, Mary and Sun all began to say "We've all got anxieties and fears."
"And, Larry, that's okay!"

Sun shared his fear of the dark.
Claude told of his fear of storms.
Mary told her fear of falling...

"So, sweet friend, what's YOURS?"

"It starts off fast.
It's EVAPORATION time
My worries heat up
as we head for the sky."

"Everyone is flying,
Moving fast ALL AROUND..."
"IT'S HARD TO STAY CALM WITH
MY FEET OFF THE GROUND."

CONDENSATION!
It's colder and slower, creating a cloud.
Vapor had space...
But now, there's a CROWD!

But next phase,
we've gotten too heavy together.
...AS PRECIPITATION WE FALL
...as some kind of weather.

"Fear and worry are heavy, Larry, anxiety is real big too"

"Let's try to figure out a way to make them a little lighter for you!"

"I know that fears can make you angry. And sometimes... even sad."

"Fears are meant to keep us safe, but sometimes they feel SO bad."

"Your tummy may have butterflies, it hurts or you may feel sick."

"But, You're SO brave, you don't need to hide, let's teach you some cool new tricks!"

Claude came up and said to Larry,...

"If it starts to storm, I'll take **deep breaths**, and **relax** holding my favorite **teddy**. "

It's loud and bright, but we have a **plan** so we will always be **ready**!"

Sun told Larry about the dark, that it made him worry at night.

"I've got my **nightlight**, my friend 'The Moon'. When she glows, it's a little more bright!"

"My family also says to me,
"Fear of the unknown..it happens alot."
"Our minds can make up scary stories.
" Replace it with a funny thought!"

"Don't forget! You ARE the SUN!"
"I only glow because of you."
"You're brighter and braver than you think.
"...all of your friends are, too!"

"Don't forget about us, Larry! A buddy close by makes it better...

Remember, you've got all of us by your side, on your flight, in the crowds, and through the stormy weather!"

Larry was stuck in a cycle of thinking
That made each day so hard.
...He felt like he was sinking.

Like the importance of water
For all living things...

...Positive thinking matters too.
because of the happiness it brings!

He has support, he knows
he's
strong,
and keeps his friends
close by.
He didn't
just change how he sees
his
job,
but how he sees his
wonderful life.

BELIEVE IN YOURSELF.

YOU ARE BRAVER THAN THOSE WORRIES.

YOU ARE MORE COURAGEOUS THAN YOU KNOW.

YOU ARE STRONGER THAN YOUR FEARS.

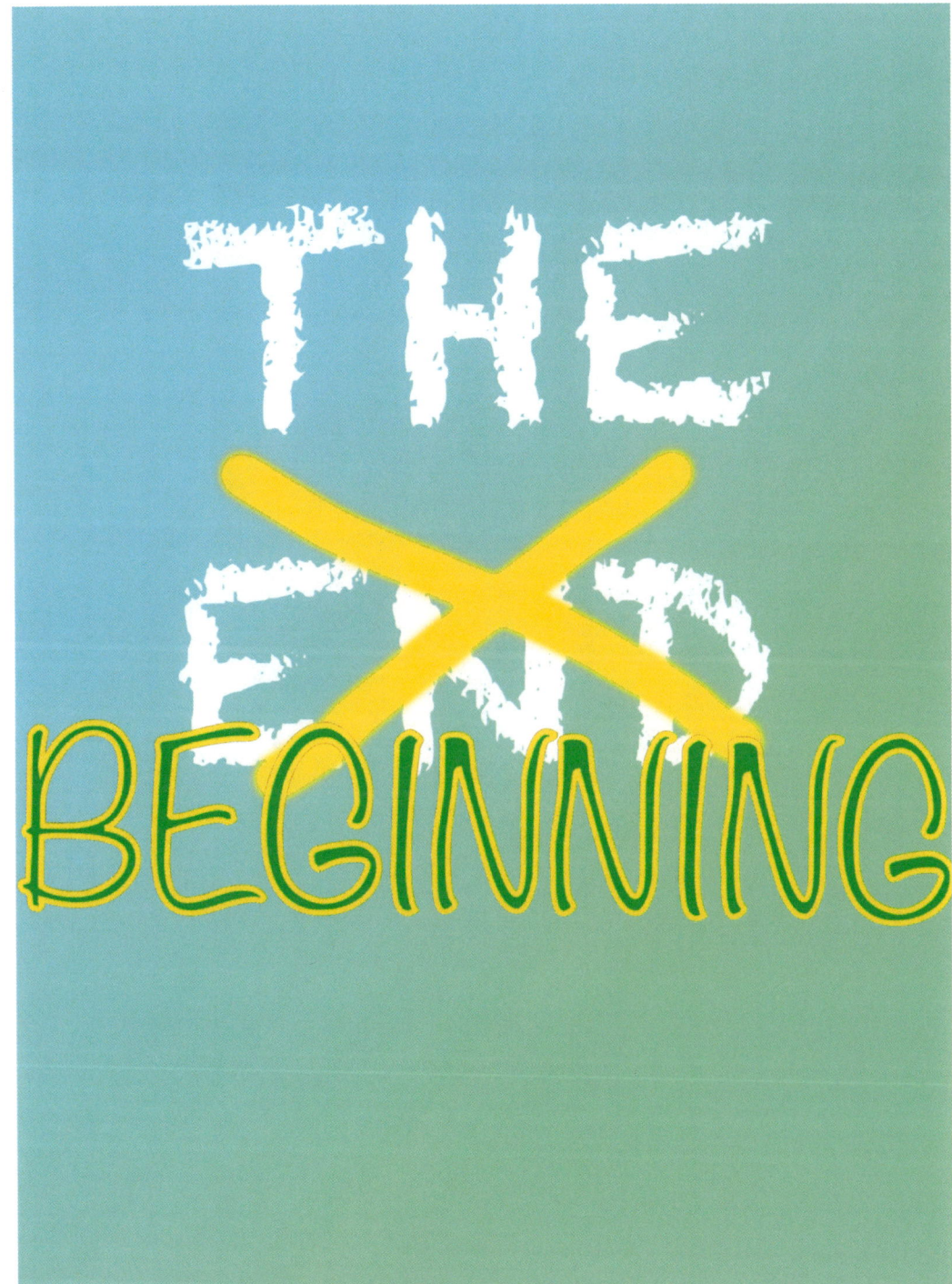

Made in the USA
Coppell, TX
29 April 2024

31832970R00021